MW00877152

A SECOND SHOT

Alex Kuskowski

SADDLEBACK
EDUCATIONAL PUBLISHING

DISTRICT ⑬

Before the Snap

Down and Out

Fighting the Legend

The Handoff

Hit Just Right

Line Up

No Easy Race

A Second Shot

Taking Control

Wings

SADDLEBACK
EDUCATIONAL PUBLISHING
www.sdlback.com

Copyright © 2012 by Saddleback Educational Publishing
All rights reserved. No part of this book may be reproduced
in any form or by any means, electronic or mechanical,
including photocopying, recording, scanning, or by any
information storage and retrieval system, without the
written permission of the publisher. SADDLEBACK
EDUCATIONAL PUBLISHING and any associated
logos are trademarks and/or registered trademarks of
Saddleback Educational Publishing.

ISBN-13: 978-1-61651-580-5
ISBN-10: 1-61651-580-5
eBook: 978-1-61247-250-8

Printed in the U.S.A.

19 18 17 16 15   6 7 8 9 10

1

"Yo. Little Bro! Move it or lose it!" Wallace McKnight yelled. He grabbed his backpack.

Wallace went out the door. His mom said to wait for Miles. But Wallace was in a rush. Today was a big day. The first day at a stupid new school. The first day to prove his basketball skills. Wallace couldn't be late.

Wallace walked down the street. He did not wait for Miles. Miles was twelve. He could walk by himself. He'd be fine.

"Wallace! Wall-*ace*!" His little brother's voice came from behind him.

Wallace stopped walking. "What?" Wallace said without looking.

"The bus stop is over here!" Miles said.

Wallace turned. Miles stood at the bus stop. He grinned at Wallace. He thought he was so smart.

Next to Miles was a girl. She had curly hair. She was the prettiest girl Wallace had ever seen.

"I was just takin' a walk," Wallace bluffed. "Waiting for your lazy ass."

The girl cocked her hip. Then she yawned. She wasn't fooled.

Wallace walked over to Miles. He whispered, "Who's that?"

The girl said, "*That* is Tasha Young. Your next-door neighbor. I was at the block party last night. You didn't come. You woulda met me if you had. Instead you were off playin' basketball."

Wallace blushed. Then he shrugged. "Be easy, Tasha. Just working on my baller moves. I can be your star player. Give you a reason to go to the games."

"Uh-huh. Well you'd better watch out, new kid. There's already a star player at Northeast High. His name is Deron Ford."

"Don't worry. It's all gravy. I seen guys who think they be cool. My game will leave them cold. Cold as you are hot."

Wallace leaned against the bus stop sign. His shoulder slid off. He fell on his butt. So much for being cool.

Miles laughed. "Smooth, bro!" he said.

Tasha giggled. She gave him a real smile. She was even prettier when she smiled. She helped him up. Wallace felt his heart race. Maybe he still had a chance.

She said, "Deron is this year's LeBron. Maybe you are good. If you're half as good as you say maybe you'll make the team."

"Then he'll get to see you dance!" Miles said.

"Dance? What dance?" Wallace was lost.

"That's right. I don't need no man. I got my own reason to go to the games," Tasha told him. "I'm captain of the dance team. Though I wouldn't mind bringing Miles as my date." She winked at Miles.

The bus pulled up. The door opened. Miles went up the steps. Tasha followed him.

"Are you coming?" she called to Wallace. "I'll show you 'round school. Can't do that if you're here."

The bus doors began to close. Wallace tripped over his feet hurrying to get on.

2

BRRRRRRRRRING!

The bell rang for lunch. Wallace walked out of class. He waved goodbye to some girls. They heard he was a basketball player. They were fighting over who got to sit by him. None were as pretty as Tasha.

Wallace turned the corner. He realized he was lost. Again. This was the third time today. At least no one cared if he was late for lunch. Well, he cared. Boy, was he hungry. Breakfast was forever ago. His bag lunch sounded better than ever.

Wallace looked around. Was his locker on the right or left?

"Oof." Wallace walked into a wall. He backed up. It wasn't a wall. It was two huge guys.

He'd run into the biggest guys at school. What were their names? Jordan Walker and E-something. Emerson? Edward?

"Where do you think you're going, man?" Jordan cracked his knuckles.

Wallace stood his ground. It was an accident. "Just looking for my locker, cos," he said. "Didn't mean trouble."

"Don't get fresh with me."
Jordan's face was mean. He frowned
at Wallace. "You're that new kid.
Wallace? The one who's been
shooting off his mouth. 'Bout joining
the basketball team?"

"So? Whatcha sayin'?" These guys
weren't even on the team.

"We're friends of Deron. He's the
best 'round here. You catch that? He
averages 30 points and six assists.
Per game, fool. In his free time he's
got ESPN on the line. You feel me?"

"I feel you. Doesn't mean I won't
try." Wallace was angry. No one had
ever talked to him this way. At his
old school they loved him. He'd been
a star. The star. He hadn't averaged
30 points though. Maybe Deron was

good. Wallace still wasn't going to be bullied.

"Since you don't play, I'll tell you. Ball is a team sport," Wallace said, "I'll only make him better. So lay off, Emerson. Or whatever your name is."

"The name's Emmitt. Emmitt Dunn." Emmitt pushed him. Wallace hit the wall. Emmitt walked away. "Remember it, new kid."

Wallace was worried. This was nothing like his old school. He wasn't giving up basketball. Not for bullies. Not for anyone. He messed up at his old school. This was his last shot. He'd just have to watch his back.

3

"Let's see what you got, kid. I don't take walk-ons." The voice boomed around the locker room. It was Mr. Adams, the basketball coach.

Mr. Adams was the best thing about this school. He'd brought the school three championship titles. He was the reason Deron was here. Otherwise he'd be at some fancy prep school.

But Mr. Adams didn't take lip from no one. Wallace was still going to give Mr. Adams as good as he got.

"We might have a problem then, Coach." Wallace tied his trainers. They were falling apart. Wallace couldn't afford new ones. That's how the old trouble had started.

"It's Mr. Adams till you make the team, McKnight. And why might we have a problem?" Mr. Adams threw a ball at Wallace.

Wallace caught the ball with one hand. He began spinning it. The ball jumped from fingertip to fingertip. Mr. Adams's eyebrows went up.

"Because this tryout? It's gonna be a cakewalk, Coach," Wallace said. He grinned.

Mr. Adams rolled his eyes. But he smiled. "See how you feel in three hours, son. Now drop that ball. Start running laps."

Wallace didn't complain. He wanted to make the team. Three hours of drills wouldn't stop him. It wouldn't get in his way. Not even close.

Wallace worked his way through the tryout. He watched the team come in. They practiced around him. Most of them were good. Some were really good. No one was better than him.

Practice ended. Wallace was tired. He was covered in sweat. He was sure he'd made the team. He started to leave.

"One more thing, Wallace," Mr. Adams said. "I want to see you play."

"No problem, Coach!" Wallace grabbed a ball. He showed off his best footwork. He made some great shots too.

"Stop! Wallace!" Mr. Adams yelled. "I want to see a scrimmage. One-on-one with Deron."

The rest of the team stopped. Everyone wanted to see this.

Wallace looked over at Deron. Deron was six feet ten inches tall. Wallace was only average height. Just over six feet. Most guys would never measure up. This was his chance to prove himself.

They started playing. They both had good moves. Both of them made some tough shots. But Deron made more shots than Wallace.

Wallace was losing. He wasn't sure what to do. But he wasn't going to give up. Not without a fight.

It was his ball. Quickly, Wallace dodged around Deron. Then he took the ball to the rim for a layup. Deron missed the block. The ball went in.

Wallace dropped his hands to his knees. He was panting. He was also still losing.

"Good job! That's enough, boys," Mr. Adams called. "Wallace, you're on the team. Be here every day. On time, son."

"Thanks, Coach!" Wallace said. "You can count on me." He took a drink of water.

The others on the team whooped. Wallace had impressed them.

"Yo!" Deron yelled. Wallace turned back. Deron's smile surprised Wallace. "I'm Deron." Deron held out a fist. Wallace looked at it. He bumped it back. "You're the new kid, right? I heard you got some mad skills."

"Yeah. Name's Wallace. You'd better believe it. I'll bring it here too." Deron seemed nice. But his friends were jerks. Wallace didn't know what to think.

"Coach is impressed. So am I."

Wallace shrugged. Deron was cool. Maybe it wouldn't be that bad here.

4

"High five, McKnight! No way we can lose now!" A teammate held up a hand in the hallway.

It was the next day. Wallace was sore but happy. Word had spread about his game with Deron. All of the basketball players were excited. It was his third high five that day.

Wallace saw Deron in the hallway before lunch.

"Yo, McKnight. Your game yesterday was hard-core. You're chill. Come sit at the team's table."

Wallace didn't hesitate. "That'd be cool," he said.

They walked to the table. All the guys were in basketball jerseys. Wallace was nervous.

"What *up*? How 'bout some recognition for my new boy here?" Deron called.

The guys turned. "Yo, McKnight's here!" They gave Wallace fist bumps and high fives. Wallace sat down. He opened his lunch bag. Maybe this place could be cool.

Jordan and Emmitt walked up to the table. They glared at Wallace. He ignored them.

Deron turned to his friends. "Hey, boys. You meet my new wingman?"

"We've met," Wallace muttered. He didn't look up.

"Whatever, Deron." Jordan pushed Wallace over. He sat next to Deron. Emmitt sat on Deron's other side. "So, you hear about Randall?" Jordan said. "He got nabbed stealing some beers."

"Damned fool," Deron said.

Jordan poked Wallace with his elbow. He said, "What about you, Knighty? You ever swipe anything? Or are you too scared of the po-lice?"

Wallace wasn't going to let Jordan win. Not in front of the team. "Back off, Walker. I've forgotten more hot stuff than you'll ever see."

Jordan and Emmitt laughed. They didn't believe him.

"I just got off probation. I walked off with tons of swag before that. I even got a car once," Wallace boasted.

He'd only stolen three things. It was the car that had gotten him probation.

"Prove it," Emmitt said.

Tasha waved at Wallace from across the room. He didn't want to sit with these guys anymore. He stood up.

"Take a look at my backpack. Now I'm off to see some other hot stuff you couldn't handle." He moved toward Tasha. The guys watched him walk away.

The backpack wasn't stolen. He had to return that one. These guys didn't have to know that though.

"Hey, Tasha. What up?" Wallace asked.

Tasha frowned. "I was gonna ask how you like the team, but ..."

"But what?" Wallace asked.

"Stay away from Jordan and Emmitt, okay? They are bad news. They got a kid arrested once."

Wallace shrugged. "Nothing I can't handle."

"Well ain't nobody gonna handle you. If you join 'em, I don't even want to talk." Tasha was angry. She walked away.

Wallace was confused. Why was Tasha so upset?

5

"Shoot and hustle, boys!" Coach yelled. Practice was almost over.

Everyone was tired. They had a game Friday. They were shooting to get the start. They'd been at it an hour. Eight players were left.

Wallace shot the ball. *Swish!* He could do this all day.

Coach nodded. "Great release, McKnight," he said.

Deron shot. It was a perfect three-pointer. No effort at all. It was why NBA scouts sat in the bleachers. The next three shooters missed. Everyone sighed. They were done.

Practice had run late. Wallace quickly grabbed his gear. Then he ran for the bus stop. A bus was just leaving. "Damn!" Wallace muttered. "I missed it."

"Hey, McKnight," Deron called. "Need a lift?"

"Yeah. That'd be sweet." Wallace caught up with Deron.

They walked to Deron's car. It was an old Chevy. Jordan and Emmitt were there. They lit a joint.

"Look, man," Deron said. "Get that away from me. If a scout saw…"

"Hey, we know the rules. We won't let no one see nothin'." Jordan stamped out the joint.

"We're gonna check out some fly kicks. You interested?" Emmitt asked.

"Sure!" said Deron. "You in, McKnight?"

Wallace was torn. He liked Deron. But he didn't trust Emmitt or Jordan. They were trouble.

"I don't know…" Wallace started.

"Don't be a punk," Jordan said.

"It's not like they have anything on them. Right guys?" Deron looked at the guys.

"Yeah. We don't want a repeat of William Young," Emmitt said.

"William Young? He Tasha's bro?" Wallace asked.

"Cousin," Deron answered shortly. "He's in juvie for possession."

"Yeah, he's my man!" Emmitt whooped.

"It was your fault!" Deron shook his head. "They got busted. Will took the fall for Emmitt. He got an extra six months."

Wallace understood why Tasha didn't like these guys.

"Well, you wanna go? Or do you wanna talk about it like girls?" Jordan asked.

Deron sighed. "Let's go. You in, McKnight?"

What harm could it do? They were just looking at shoes.

"Yeah. I'm in."

6

They stopped in front of the store.
Wallace got a bad feeling. He'd told
his mom he'd come right home. He
was two hours late. What if she
found out? He was still grounded
from before.

"So how hard was it to steal
stuff?" Jordan asked.

"Easy if it's small," Wallace
bluffed. "Just remove the tags. Then

stick it in a bag. It's the cars that are a big deal."

"Can you hot-wire a car too?" Deron asked. He was impressed.

"Sure I can." Wallace couldn't. His best friend did that. His friend who was in juvie now. "But let's check out those kicks first."

They got out of the car. Emmitt grabbed a bag from the backseat. They went into the store.

The clerk glared at them. "We're closing soon. Not like you'll buy anything," he sneered. He eyed Emmitt's bag suspiciously.

Wallace was annoyed. They'd just walked into the store! They weren't doing anything. What was this guy's problem?

Jordan and Emmitt ignored the clerk. They cracked jokes. They started throwing shoes like footballs. Wallace walked the other way.

Deron was in heaven. "Aw, man. Do you see these?" He held up a shoe with bright orange laces. "I've wanted these more than anything." He pulled a picture from his pocket. It was an ad for the shoes.

"So buy 'em," Wallace suggested.

Deron looked at his ratty trainers. "Got no cash. All my money goes into that clunker." He pointed to his beat-up car.

"If you've 'got no cash,' I suggest you get outta here. I will call the police on your asses." The clerk had snuck up behind them.

"We done nothing wrong," Wallace said.

"Yeah. But what about them?" He jerked his thumb at Jordan and Emmitt. "You got five minutes before I call the cops. And who you think they'll believe? Me? Or a bunch of rowdy boys?" He walked away.

"What a jerk," Deron said. He shook his head.

"We weren't doing nothing!" Wallace was angry.

"It's always like this with those two." Deron looked at Emmitt and Jordan.

"Why do you hang with them?" Wallace asked. He couldn't figure it out. Deron was cool. He didn't need those guys.

"They're friends of Will's. He asked me to watch out for them. He can't while he's locked up." Deron looked upset. "Haven't done a good job." He started toward Emmitt and Jordan.

"Wait." Wallace grabbed his arm. "I've got a friend in juvie too. You don't need their trash. Let 'em go, man."

"Can't," Deron answered.

Wallace shrugged. Then he grinned. "I got an idea."

He looked around. He saw that the clerk was busy. Then he got to work.

7

Wallace and Deron left the store laughing.

"Man, I can't believe you switched the shoes up like that!" Deron said. "It'll take hours to fix. That was chill."

"Yeah," Wallace shrugged. The clerk had deserved it. He had been mean to them. Wallace still felt a little bad, though.

"Yo. Wait up, guys!" Jordan and Emmitt caught up to them.

"You forgot your bag in the store," Emmitt said. He gave Deron the bag.

Wallace saw an orange shoelace. It was hanging out of the bag.

"Wait. How did those shoes get in the bag?" Wallace asked.

"I put them there," Jordan laughed. "Just like you said before. Easy. A present for my man Deron."

"Well you gotta return 'em. I told you. I don't do that stuff anymore," Wallace said. He was angry.

"What is your problem? It's just shoes, man," Emmitt said.

"My problem? My problem is I just got off probation. I'm not doing this again!" Wallace yelled.

Deron stopped. "It's not like it's a car. They're good shoes. I'll play better on Friday." He took the shoes out to look at them. A bag of pot fell out too.

"What! You put the drugs in there too?" Wallace was really mad now. "Man, I don't want any part of this." Wallace started walking away.

Then they heard the sirens. The police were very close. They were just around the corner.

Jordan said, "Oh, naw, man. I won't get caught either. I'll see you guys later." He ran down the street. He turned into an alley.

"Yeah, you guys are on your own. You got a car. Use it." Emmitt ran after Jordan.

Wallace was stunned. He just stood there. Deron panicked. "I can't. I can't get caught with this."

He stuffed the shoes and pot into the bag. He tossed the bag to Wallace. He got in his car. "I'm sorry, bro. This is my future." Then he drove off.

Wallace held the bag. He was in shock. He watched Deron's car speed away.

Wallace didn't want to get arrested either. He looked around. There was a large trash can by the building. He shoved the bag behind it.

He saw the flashing lights. He thought about running. But it was too late to run now.

8

Wallace was in jail. Not real jail. Yet. He was in the police station.

They police called his mom. She was angry. He heard her on the phone. Everyone heard her. She and his stepdad would kick him out for sure. He put his head down.

"Wallace McKnight. Want to tell me what's up? Why did you have stolen shoes?" Officer Baker asked.

He was nice. Nicer than the other cops. The ones who arrested him before. Baker got Wallace a drink. He didn't seem to think Wallace was guilty.

Wallace held up his hands. He wasn't a rat. Jordan and Emmitt deserved it. Deron didn't. Wallace would keep his mouth shut. For now.

"What about the drugs? Mr. McKnight?"

Wallace's mouth opened. He was scared. He looked over. Jordan and Emmitt glared. They had been caught near the store.

They weren't sitting far away. If Wallace said anything they'd know. They might come after him. Wallace closed his mouth.

Baker said, "With your record this could go to trial. No judge will believe you're innocent. Not with your priors. You have to say something."

Wallace was quiet. He heard Emmitt across the room. He was talking to another officer. "It was all Wallace. I told him not to steal the shoes."

"Yeah. It was all Wallace. I didn't do nothing," Jordan said.

Wallace stood up. "That's a lie! You're both liars!" he yelled. "I never touched them shoes. Or the drugs neither!"

The officer yelled at Jordan and Emmitt. "Mr. Walker! Mr. Dunn! Please wait your turn."

Baker grabbed Wallace. He pushed Wallace into his chair.

"Sit down!" Baker said. Wallace shrugged off his hand. He was ready. They asked for a fight.

"Beating them down won't help. Think of your case," Baker said.

Wallace clenched his hands. He couldn't let Emmitt get away with it. But it was two against one.

"Say something. If you don't, we'll send you away. You'll go to juvie. The trial would be later. I don't think you did it," Baker said. He was trying to help.

"It's two against one," was all Wallace could say.

"They have records too. Someone will listen." But Wallace knew no one would listen. Not his parents. Not the judge. No one. Except maybe this cop. Would it be enough?

"I … I …" Wallace started to say. He thought of Deron. His future. Wallace couldn't ruin that. "Can't."

Wallace put his head in his hands. His mom would be here soon. He was in real trouble this time. What was he going to do?

9

Suddenly the doors opened. It was Deron! Why was he here? He got away! The store clerk came in too.

"Uncle Joe," Deron said. He walked up to Officer Baker.

"Deron! What are you doing here?" Baker was surprised.

Emmitt and Jordan exploded. "Hey! Deron! My man!" they yelled. "Come to spring us?"

Wallace was doomed. He closed his eyes. He waited. Deron was going to say Wallace did it. It was all over. No basketball. No Tasha. No home. Deron was quiet. When would he get this over with?

Deron took a breath. "It was my fault, Uncle Joe. Wallace didn't do it."

Jordan and Emmitt shut up.

Baker looked at Deron. "Are you telling me that you stole the shoes? And the drugs were yours? You've never stolen anything, son."

"I didn't steal. But I didn't stop Jordan and Emmitt. Not like Wallace tried to do." Deron hung his head.

"You know this is serious, Deron." Baker wouldn't let Deron off the hook. Even if he was his nephew.

Deron nodded. "I know. But I gotta be a man. Own up."

"After all we've done for you? You turn your back on us? On your friends?" Emmitt said.

Deron stood over Emmitt and Jordan. "You ain't my friends. My *friend* is in jail because of you."

"It's two against two. Can't prove nothing," Jordan exploded.

"I've got a clean record," Deron responded.

"Well. Is there anything else you'd like to say?" Baker asked Deron.

"Yeah, actually. The store clerk knows the bag was Emmitt's. We didn't touch it."

Everyone turned to the clerk. He nodded and walked over. He kept

looking back at Emmitt and Jordan.
They were very unhappy.

"What's your name?" Baker asked.

"It's Mike. Mike Harris," he said.
"They came in together, but it was
his bag." Mike pointed to Emmitt.
"I saw them fighting about it. After
they left the store. It's all on tape
too." Mike gave the tape to Baker.

"Well that seals it." Baker tapped
his desk. He looked at Deron. "You
did the right thing, Deron. But
you're still in a heap of trouble here.
At home too."

Deron nodded. "I know. Juvie,
right?"

Wallace put his head down. He
couldn't believe it. Another friend in
juvie? What about the team?

Baker laughed. "No, son. I think you'll be grounded so hard you'll wish for juvie. And you'll do community service. Volunteer for it. Then I think the charges can be dropped."

Wallace took a deep breath. Good.

Baker turned to Wallace. "Finish your statement, Wallace. Then you're free to go."

Wallace wasn't in trouble? He smiled. Finally things were going his way!

"But wait for your mom," Baker continued. "She can take you home."

Wallace stopped smiling. His mom was still going to be mad. But he could handle that. Anything was better than jail.

10

Wallace twirled a basketball. He had his team jersey on. He felt proud. But he was nervous too.

The crowd was cheering out in the gym. His mom was there. So was Tasha. She was with the dance team.

The players waited in the locker room. Deron and Coach Adams were late. Everyone was quiet. Could they start the game without them?

It was five minutes to game time. Then Deron came in.

"My man! Where you been?" Wallace called.

"Working out community service stuff. Coach had an idea. Something better than picking up trash," Deron said. He shrugged. "I'll help coach in the kids league."

"Doesn't seem bad. My little bro plays in that league," Wallace said.

Deron laughed. "Oh, I know! He'll be my worst nightmare," he said. He really thought it would be fun. But he wouldn't say so.

"Better than my weekends," Wallace muttered. "Mom grounded me for life. I can barely leave the house."

"Mamma McKnight!" Deron laughed. "She wants to keep you to herself. Away from the neighbor."

"Who? Tasha? What did you hear?" Wallace's heart thumped.

"I heard that girl is sweet," Deron paused. Wallace glared at Deron. He didn't like Tasha. Did he?

"Sweet on you," Deron finished.

"Really? You think?" Wallace hoped so. Tasha had been nice to him. She brought Wallace cookies. For the game, she'd said.

Deron whistled. "I saw them treats at lunch. Looks like you sweet on her too, cos. Who wouldn't be, though? She is hot!"

Wallace threw the basketball. "You ain't going for my girl, now?"

Deron caught it. "Naw. Single life for me. Gotta spread the love."

"Uh-huh." Wallace wasn't sure. Deron could get any girl in school. What if he changed his mind?

Coach came in. "All right, guys! Let's go get 'em!" They headed for the gym. Everyone was psyched.

"Seriously, man. Won't touch her," Deron said. They moved to the doors. "Can't get you angry. Uncle Joe says I gotta keep you 'round. You'll keep me in line."

Wallace laughed. "Me? Keep *you* in line? How 'bout I get you a spot to shoot at the line. But tell my mom. She might unground me. Let me do something. Not that basketball and school isn't something."

"Jordan and Emmitt are gone. I need someone new to beat down," Deron joked. He said he wasn't sorry about Jordan and Emmitt. They got what they deserved. Wallace was glad. He and Deron were good friends now.

"How 'bout we beat down the competition first?" Wallace said.

"A team with me *and* you? This won't even *be* a competition." Deron grinned.

Wallace and Deron opened the gym doors. The crowd cheered. Deron was right. This wouldn't be a competition. It would be a cakewalk.